Shander

Walt Disney
The Sword in the Stone

Twin Books

Many, many centuries ago, England was still covered with thick forests and London was only a small town. The king died and left no heir to fill the throne of England. But one morning, the citizens of London found a magic sword planted in an anvil, placed on a stone. On its hilt was written a mysterious message:

"Only he who can remove this sword from the stone is worthy of the crown of England."

A miracle! All the men in the kingdom, old and young, rich and poor, strong and weak, flocked to London to try and pull the sword out of the anvil. Not one succeeded; England was left without a king.

The sword in the stone was soon forgotten … until a magician by the name of Merlin changed the fate of England.

3

Merlin the Magician lived in the middle of the forest. Everyday he fought with his creaky well. "What a nuisance, these Middle Ages!" he would mutter. "To think it will be another thousand years before we invent running water!"

He had seen in his crystal ball that today he would have a visitor, and, since in England one must serve tea to guests, the magician continued to struggle with the well.

While Merlin was getting ready for his visitor, the two sons of Lord Hector, who lived in a nearby castle, went hunting. Kay, Hector's first son, was tall, strong and very stupid; Wart was Hector's second son and had been adopted. He was skinny and quick. Kay always brought him along on a hunt because he was very good at driving out the game.

As they were walking, a stag leaped out of the forest in front of them.

"Ah-hah!" said Kay. "Just follow my arrow! We'll have good meat for supper tonight!"

Kay drew and fired, but his arrow hit a tree instead. The stag was much too quick for him.

"Wart! Go get my arrow," he ordered and without waiting, he left. Wart climbed up the tree and reached over for the arrow … *crack*! The branch gave way and Wart crashed through the roof of a tiny cottage hidden under the tree! He landed right in Merlin's home.

"Right on time," said Merlin. "I was expecting you!"

"Is this the proper way to pay a visit?" squalled a bad-tempered owl perched on Merlin's hat.

"Welcome to my home! My name is Merlin and this is Archimedes," said Merlin, pointing to the owl.

"He isn't stuffed?" asked Wart, puzzled.

"Stuffed?! Stuffed yourself !" squawked Archimedes, offended.

Wart had just met the most sensitive owl in the forest.

Merlin poured Wart a cup of tea.

"Look at the steam coming out of the teapot. In about ten centuries, Denis Papin will invent the steam engine …. But that's another story. What's your name, my boy?" asked Merlin.

"My name is Arthur, sir," replied Wart, "but everybody calls me Wart."

"What do you want to be when you grow up, Arthur?" asked Merlin.

"I want to be a knight's squire," answered the boy firmly.

"Don't you want to learn and read big books? I am a magician and I know a lot of things. I'll come to your castle and give you an education," suggested Merlin.

But Wart was not convinced of Merlin's magical abilities. The old man seemed crazy! Merlin decided to pack his bags anyway. At his command, all the books, chairs, tables, plates and dishes, carpets and musical instruments squeezed into his tiny bag.

"Do you believe me now?" Merlin asked a very startled Wart.

12

"What was the big round ball you packed in your bag?" Wart asked Merlin.

"Ah, very good! An excellent beginning! This ball is a globe that represents the Earth." answered the magician.

"The Earth?" interrupted Wart. "That can't be! The Earth is flat!"

"No! In the twentieth century people will travel around the Earth. I am not crazy, just a little ahead of our times."

"Because you are a magician?" asked the boy.

"Magic can't solve every single problem," grunted Merlin, then added with a twinkle in his eye, "even magicians can get their beards caught in doors!"

"Come on, my boy! Show me the way to your castle!" said Merlin.

"Don't you know the way?" asked Wart.

"I don't know everything! Hum … let's first cross this pond. Follow me!" he ordered. Much to Wart's surprise, Merlin walked *on* the water! The boy was even more amazed when he found that he too could walk on the water.

It was lucky that Wart could follow Merlin across the pond because a hungry wolf was close on their trail, squinting with pleasure at the thought of having Merlin and Wart for lunch.

Merlin had noticed the wolf behind them. He ran to a precipice and jumped over it. Wart followed him with a great big leap but the wolf, afraid of heights, did not dare to jump. He howled with rage as he saw his lunch set off on the soft green grass on the other side of the precipice.

By the time the wolf had found his way around the precipice, Merlin and Wart were very close to the castle.

"Never go near castles!" the wolf's grandmother had warned him. "They are too dangerous for wolves!" His grandmother's words cut his appetite short ... he had remembered just in time!

In the castle's great hall, Lord Hector was drinking to Kay's good health. Kay had just gulped down fourteen appetizers and now waited for the main dishes!

Wart stepped forward and introduced Merlin.

"Welcome to my home, Lord Marvin!" stuttered Hector.

"Merlin!" corrected the magician.

"Yes, yes, Marvin. What can I do for you?" asked Hector.

"I would like to instruct this young man," replied Merlin. "He is very gifted!"

"What?" laughed Hector. "Gifted? He is only gifted to wash dishes, this boy!"

"He wants to become a knight's squire," insisted Merlin.

"Certainly not!" bellowed Hector. "This boy belongs in the kitchen. Now leave my castle immediately!"

Merlin raised his magical wand and whispered a very ancient magical formula: "Abracadabrus, abracadabri, abracadabro, abracadabra!"

Within seconds snow started to fall on Kay and Hector.

24

The snowflakes were as big as partridge eggs! Very quickly the hall looked like the cold steppes of central Siberia.

"Enough! Enough!" Hector cried out. "Please stop the snow! I promise I'll let you teach the boy, Marvin!"

"Thank you," said Merlin, and he lowered his magical wand. "Where can I stay?"

Lord Hector did not want to live near Merlin. After some thought he offered Merlin the north tower of the castle, which shook and rattled and threatened to tumble down at each thunderstorm. Merlin said nothing but Archimedes was insulted.

"Quiet, Archimedes! Put away our books!" ordered Merlin.

"But it rains on the table and you hate wet sugar in your tea! This is scandalous!" grumbled the owl.

"Archimedes, enough!" said Merlin. "This tower is now our new home, understood? Let's put away these books in a dry place!"

Every morning Wart climbed up the wobbly staircase that led to Merlin's tower, and studied with his teacher. But one morning he was late. Merlin was looking out his window when he saw a horseman gallop across the the castle's drawbridge.

"How strange!" he mused. "He can't be the mailman delivering the newspaper — the first edition of *The Times* won't come out for another twelve centuries!"

Just then Wart burst into the room. He was very excited. "A messenger has come from London! There is going to be a tournament and whoever wins will be crowned king of England. Kay wants to go … I'll be his squire!"

Merlin doubted that Kay would win. But every day Wart helped train his brother. He built a puppet knight on a horse.

"I'll hide behind the puppet and at each attack I'll operate the spear," he explained to the wizard.

"Very clever, my boy, and when will this tournament take place?" asked Merlin.

"At the new year! I will go to London with Kay," answered Wart.

"Wart!" called Kay as he clunked his way across the courtyard in a heavy suit of armor. "Is the spear in place? I feel great! I will swallow this puppet in one bite!"

Merlin laughed up his sleeve; Kay could not even climb up on his horse!

The following day Wart found a huge pile of dirty dishes in the kitchen. Kay and Lord Hector had feasted again the night before.

"No training or studying for me today," sighed Wart. He ran to the tower to tell Merlin.

Merlin was very angry. "Education is more important than washing dishes!" he said. "Take me to the kitchen at once! I'll take care of this chore, my boy."

"I am going to show you the forerunner of the dishwashing machine, heh, heh, heh!" he said with a chuckle. He pointed his magical wand at a huge wooden tub, which slowly lifted off the ground. "Soap, tub!" he ordered, and the tub filled with hot soapy water. "At my command: dishes, fly! Brushes, scrub!"

Merlin was very pleased with his invention. He told Wart, "my dear boy, you no longer have anything to do here! Let's go study nature!"

While the dishes were being done with the help of magic, Merlin, Archimedes and Wart went for a walk around the castle. A calm river filled the moat around the castle to protect it from possible attacks.

"Do you know anything about the underwater world, my boy?" asked Merlin.

"Aquarius, aquaticus, fishonicus!" said Archimedes, proud of his Latin.

"No, I don't," replied Wart. "But I would love to swim like a fish!"

"Is that so?" asked Merlin with a great big smile.

Wart should never have opened his mouth! With a
touch of his wand, Merlin transformed the boy into a
fish. Wart couldn't believe his fins.

"Come on, my little fish," said Merlin, catching
hold of him. "We'll go down the river together!" And
with that, Merlin also changed into a fish.

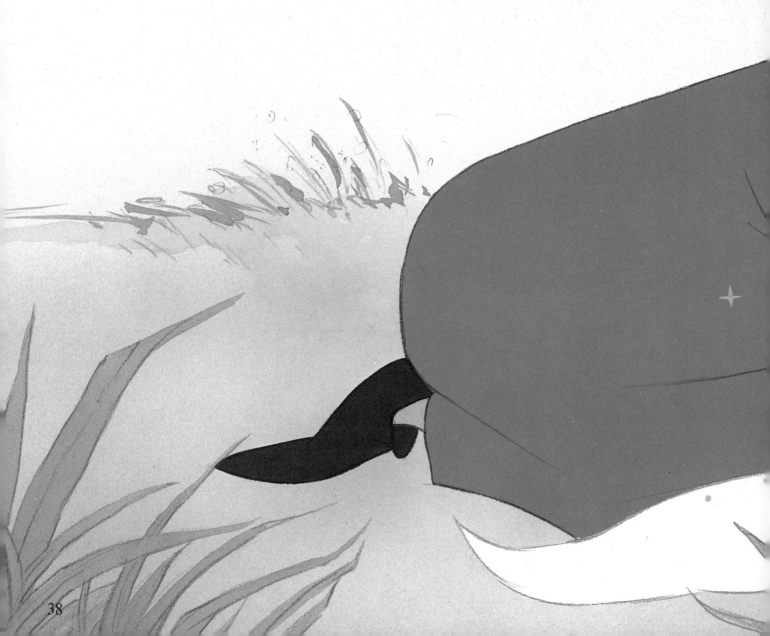

"I love being a fish!" said Wart, playing in the water. But the river, like the land, was full of dangerous and hungry creatures.

"Watch out, a pike!" called out Merlin as the predator fish glided into view. Merlin quickly hid beneath a knight's helmet stuck in the bottom of the river. The pike headed for Wart with his jaws wide open and his two rows of formidable teeth gleaming in the water.

"Quick, Wart!" yelled Merlin. "Use your dorsal fins to gain speed! Quick, swim away!"

Wart flapped his fins and wriggled his tail but there was nothing he could do. The pike was more powerful than the little inexperienced fish!

All of a sudden, Wart saw a lost arrow stuck in some algae. With his tail he pushed the arrow into the monster's open mouth so the pike could not close his jaws!

Merlin was very proud of his pupil's cleverness.

The pike was very angry. With one loud snap, he broke the arrow in two and chased after Wart even faster. Luckily Archimedes was flying over the clear river, watching over his friend. In a last effort to escape the angry pike, the little fish leapt out of the water. Archimedes caught him in mid-air and brought him to the shore. Wart was at last safe!

Merlin joined the two on land, and struggled to get the helmet off his head as Wart gasped for air.

Archimedes was incensed. "May the devil eat you!" he said to Merlin (the worst of insults for an owl). "Change that fish back into a boy immediately! *I* am going to dry my feathers at the castle!" With that, Archimedes flapped away.

Wart was changed back into a little boy. "How long have we been gone?" he asked, worried that he had stayed away from the kitchen too long.

Meanwhile, inside the castle, Lord Hector and Kay called for Wart, but the boy was nowhere to be found. They went to the kitchen to find him but instead found Merlin's dishwashing magic in its rinsing phase!

"By Jove," said Hector. "This is sorcery!"

"The work of the devil!" agreed Kay.

"Let's fight these demoniacal dishes and plates as real men would! Attack!" ordered Hector.

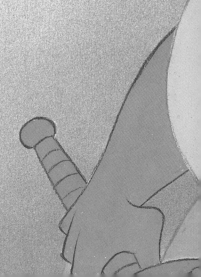

Lord Hector broke his sword swinging at the frying pans and dishes. By the time Merlin and Wart reached the kitchen, Kay had broken almost every single plate and the floor looked like the aftermath of a battle.

Merlin lifted his wand to save any dish that was left to save. Kay was very angry. "You are fired! You are no longer my squire, Wart!" he shouted at his brother.

"Excellent!" exclaimed Merlin. "Wart, let's continue with our walk!"

"In the river?" asked Wart, worried.

"No, in the woods this time!"

In the forest, Merlin and Wart changed into squirrels and climbed an oak tree.

"Ouch!" cried out Wart. "Something almost knocked me over!"

"That was an acorn. One cannot afford to underestimate the universal laws of gravity. Someone by the name of Newton will be the first to formulate them in about ten centuries. You are much too young to know that, of course!" explained Merlin.

A lady squirrel scampered up the tree and took quite a fancy to Wart.

"She wants a squirrel kiss," chuckled Merlin as he walked away. "That's obvious!"

Wart held the lady squirrel at bay wondering how he could make her understand that he was not what she thought he was, but only a little boy.

"After all, it's his problem, not mine!" thought Merlin as he hid in the foliage.

The lady squirrel was the least of Wart's problems
… the lean and hungry wolf was waiting for Wart at
the foot of the tree! He licked his chops and circled
around. Suddenly Wart's newfound friend leaped onto
the grass on the wolf's far side. Drooling at the
thought of a catch, the wolf took off after her. She led
him as far away from her new little friend as she
could! Wart was very moved by her courage.

"Merlin! Merlin!" he called out. "Help her or the
wolf will catch her!"

Taking his human form again, Merlin leaped in front
of the wolf. Frightened, the wolf ran away. Much to
the lady squirrel's disappointment, Wart also became
human.

"Don't be sad, little one!" Wart told her. "We were not meant for each other, can't you see? I hope you find another squirrel very soon who can be nicer to you than I ever could be!"

Back at the castle, Merlin decided that they had studied enough science and opted for geography. Wart was a little disoriented.

"Look at this map," started Merlin. "Everyone believes the world is as flat as a pancake. A ship sailing far enough across the sea would then fall off the edge of the world! But that is nonsense!"

"But it *is* true!" protested Wart.

"The truth, my dear boy, is that the earth is round and turns around the sun," explained the magician.

"That can't be true. Even I can see that the sun turns around the Earth!" said Wart.

"Quiet!" shouted Archimedes. "You must listen to the teacher: one learns geography from the globe, not maps!"

After the geography lesson was over, Wart practiced writing at the blackboard. Archimedes, self-elected teacher on the subject, watched him closely.

But Wart was preocuppied, and soon he asked Archimedes, "Could you teach me how to fly?"

"What for?" replied the grumpy owl.

"To see if the world is really round," was Wart's answer.

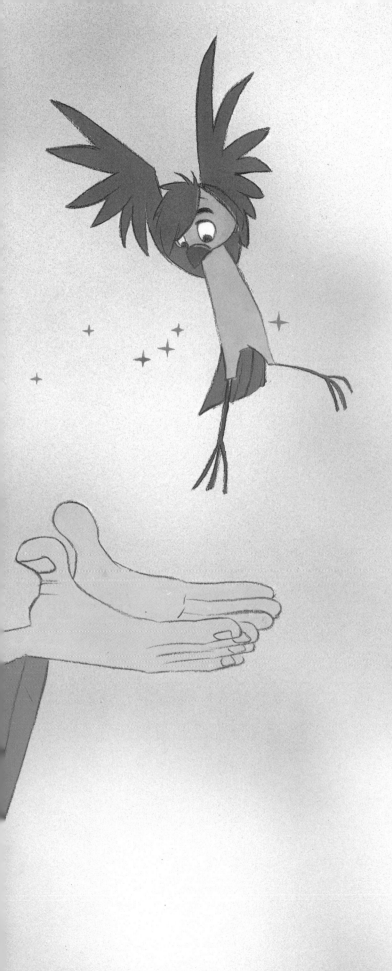

Archimedes went to
Merlin and begged him to
change Wart into a
fledgling. "I will be a good
father to him," the owl
insisted.

Merlin consented with a
laugh. He pronounced a
magical formula and Wart
felt his wings grow.

"Are you ready for
takeoff?" asked the
magician. He threw Wart up
in the air outside the
window.

"Oh! ah!" exclaimed
Wart. "It's so high!"

"Flap your wings, my
boy! That's what they're
for!" instructed Archimedes
He took his role as a father
rather seriously.

"Very good, little one!
Watch the landing!"
cautioned Archimedes.

"This is wonderful, and a
lot more fun than
swimming!" shouted Wart.

"Naturally, my dear boy,
flying is poetry in motion!
Follow me to those clouds."

"I'll follow you to the
very last one, Archimedes!"
said Wart.

Wart was to learn very quickly that the sky could be as dangerous as the river.

"Careful, an eagle!" shouted Archimedes. "Turn, boy, turn!"

Wart couldn't believe that a bird would attack another bird. But he had little time to wonder as he put all his effort into trying to turn. "Just what I don't know how to do," he muttered under his breath. He spotted a chimney below and took a nose dive for it.

Wart thought it was one of the chimneys of his father's castle. What a surprise when he landed in the fireplace of Madam Mim, the wicked witch!

"Who are you?" she barked, furious at the intrusion. "What do you want?"

"I wanted to learn how to fly, and Merlin ..."

"Who? Merlin? That old pile of rattling bones? *I* am Mim, the best sorceress in the country. Your Merlin is a clown compared to me!" she boasted.

Mim fell into a deep curtsy.

"She is truly horrible!" thought Wart.

"Don't you believe me capable of magic?" she questioned. She grew so large that she filled up the cottage and then shrunk to the size of a hairpin. Wart could barely see her.

"Am I not the best witch in the country?" she asked, showing her only tooth in a wide smile. "I am very tempted to keep you hostage. Let Merlin come and rescue you if he dares!" She burst out laughing.

Merlin appeared in the cottage immediately. He was very angry at Mim.

"I will show you, Mim!" shouted Merlin.

"No, I will show *you*!" Mim shouted back. The two enemies agreed to a duel of magic, a duel in which the only weapon was the power of *metamorphosis*.

"Let me remind you of the rules," said Mim. "Number one: it is forbidden to disappear. And number two: it is forbidden to change into animals that don't exist."

"I know that," mumbled Merlin. "I also know that you are a cheat and a liar!"

"Let's get started," laughed Mim in reply. "I can't wait to make a fool of you in front of someone!"

Mim and Merlin stood back to back, ready to take the ten steps before they could begin the duel. The count began.

"Mim! You cheated again!" shouted Merlin.

The wicked witch had transformed herself into an alligator while they were still counting the ten steps! The ugly reptile opened her jaws to swallow her prey ... Merlin!

"If that's how you want to play, fine with me!" said Merlin and he slipped into the shape of a turtle. Mim was afraid to break her teeth on the turtle's shell, so she angrily turned the turtle on its back.

Merlin was not very comfortable on his back. He couldn't get back on his legs so he changed into a hare and was off in a second. Mim quickly changed into a fox and the mad chase had begun!

The duel was quick and fierce. To escape the fox, the hare became a caterpillar! To eat the caterpillar, Mim changed into a chicken.

"Merlin, watch out for the chicken! She is going to peck at you!" Wart cried out.

The duel was most
confusing: tiger against
mouse, crab against eel,
rhinoceros against crab and
at last...

79

…ram against a rhinoceros! Merlin-the-ram butted
Mim-the-rhinoceros right into a tree! Mim couldn't
move. Humiliated and furious, she changed herself into
a fiery dragon and spat flames at her enemy.

But Merlin was not finished yet. He changed into a
virus!

Mim caught a fever and ran home to bed with a 103 degree fever and scarlet spots all over her body!

After the historic duel was over, Merlin and Wart returned to the castle. Kay was leaving with his father for the tournament in London, but his squire had fallen ill. What should he do? He couldn't go to the tournament without a squire. What a dishonor!

"I am in good health. Take me to London with you!" volunteered Wart.

"I don't have a choice, do I? All right, take my sword and put on your woolen clothes. It will snow!"

Wart was very excited, but Merlin was furious!

"A squire! What a miserable future. And to think that I educated you!" moaned Merlin. "I don't want to see this tournament. Good bye!" With that, he vanished into thin air.

Archimedes was fed up with Merlin's disappearing acts. He decided to stay with Wart and follow him to London.

"I don't like him taking holidays just like that without telling me where he goes or when he'll be back!" growled the owl along the way.

When they arrived at the tournament, Wart saw that he had forgotten Kay's sword at the inn where they had stayed the night before. But which inn was it? They all looked alike in London! Wart was anxious to find the sword in time for the tournament.

Archimedes flew over to help him. "Follow me!" he called to Wart. "I found a sword nearby. Kay is so stupid that he won't notice the difference!"

Archimedes led Wart to a large stone. On it stood an anvil and in the anvil was a sword.

"But it's an old sword!" said Wart, disappointed. "It doesn't even look like Kay's!"

"That doesn't matter. Kay is too stupid to tell them apart. Go ahead, take it!" insisted Archimedes.

Wart gently took hold of the sword.

"Pull! Don't be afraid to take it out of the anvil!" insisted Archimedes.

As if by magic, Wart slowly pulled the sword out of the anvil.

Wart was frightened. "It looks like a magical sword," he whispered. He looked around to see if the magician had played this trick on him, but saw no one.

"Merlin has nothing to do with this," assured Archimedes. "He went for a walk in the future, that madman! Don't worry about him. Take the sword to Kay. Now."

Wart did as Archimedes told him.

"Better late than never," grunted Kay when he saw them. "I would have cut off your nose if you had lost my sword!"

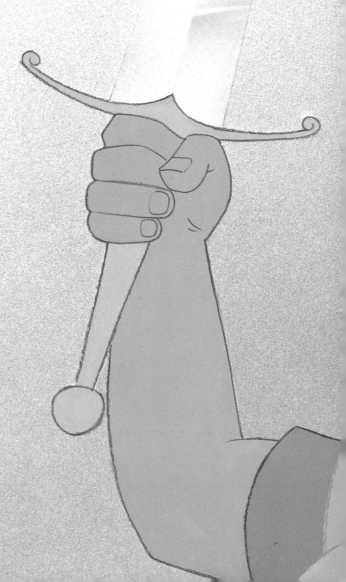

Lord Hector, however, was a little more observant than his son. He took the sword and carefully examined it.

"This is not *your* sword, Kay!" he declared. "This sword is an antique! Where did you steal it from, you little scoundrel?"

"I found it planted in an anvil on a stone," confessed Wart sheepishly.

"Planted in an anvil?" repeated Hector. "It sounds like the devil's work to me. Let's have a look!"

Wart led Hector and Kay to the anvil. Carefully, he slid the sword back into place.

Word of the long forgotten
sword soon spread across
town.

Each and every knight
came to try and pull the
sword out, but all failed.
Finally Wart stepped
forward and quietly grasped
the hilt of the sword.
Without effort he slipped it
out of the anvil.

"A miracle!" shouted the
crowd. "The boy will be
our king!"

"What is your name, my
boy?" asked a knight.

"Arthur."

"Long live Arthur, the
King of England!" cheered
the crowd.

The young boy was triumphantly carried to his future palace. In later years he would live wonderful adventures at the head of the Knights of the Round Table. But for the moment, he was very much entangled in his royal cloak and rather uncomfortable with his new authority. How he wanted Merlin to be with him! He still needed a teacher to show him how to be a king.

Merlin heard his pupil's wish and cancelled his stay in the future so abruptly that he did not have the time to change his clothes!

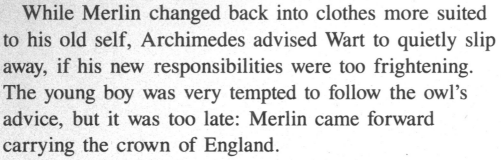

While Merlin changed back into clothes more suited to his old self, Archimedes advised Wart to quietly slip away, if his new responsibilities were too frightening. The young boy was very tempted to follow the owl's advice, but it was too late: Merlin came forward carrying the crown of England.

"Hold up your head! And stand up straight!" he said. "I hereby crown you Arthur, King of England! Remember that you will become as legendary as myself!"

When the crowning ceremony was over, Merlin returned to his cottage in the woods, and to his dusty old books. He often thought about the young king who had been his best pupil ever. "Good old King Arthur, heh, heh, heh!" he would chuckle to himself. "To think he dropped in through the roof, and almost into my cup of tea! When was that? The day before last, perhaps?"

Produced by
Twin Books
15 Sherwood Place
Greenwich, CT 16830

ISBN 1-85469-988-1

Printed in Hong Kong

1 2 3 4 5 6 7 8 9 10